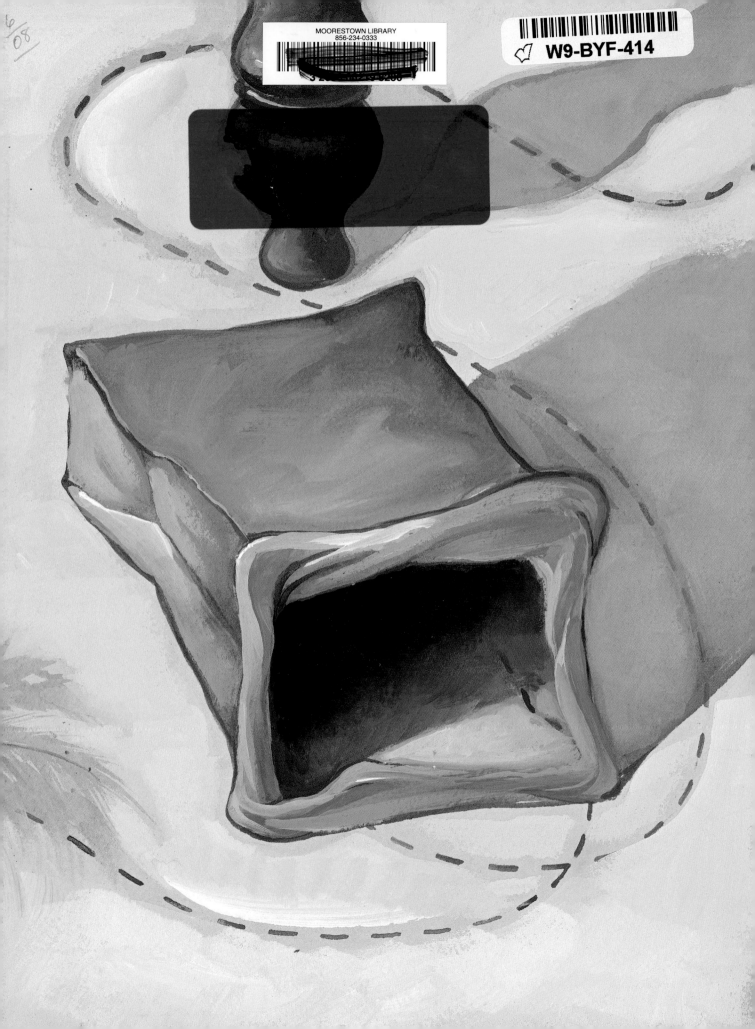

Oh, Theodore!

Guinea Pig Poems

by Susan Katz

Illustrated by Stacey Schuett

Clarion Books • New York

Clarion Books
a Houghton Mifflin Company imprint
215 Park Avenue South, New York, NY 10003
Text copyright © 2007 by Susan Katz
Illustrations copyright © 2007 by Stacey Schuett

The illustrations were executed in acrylic paint and acrylic gouache on
Arches cold-press watercolor paper.
The text was set in 17-point Coop Light.

www.clarionbooks.com

Printed in Singapore

Library of Congress Date Library of Congress Cataloging-in-Publication Data

Katz, Susan.
Oh, Theodore! : guinea pig poems / by Susan Katz ; illustrated by Stacey Schuett.
p. cm.
ISBN-13: 978-0-618-70222-0
ISBN-10: 0-618-70222-9
1. Guinea pigs–Juvenile poetry. 2. Guinea pigs as pets–Juvenile poetry.
3. Pets–Juvenile poetry. 4. Children's poetry, American. I. Schuett, Stacey. II. Title.
III. Title: Guinea pig poems.
PS3561.A775 O5 2007
811'.54–dc22   2006029205

TWP 10 9 8 7 6 5 4 3 2 1

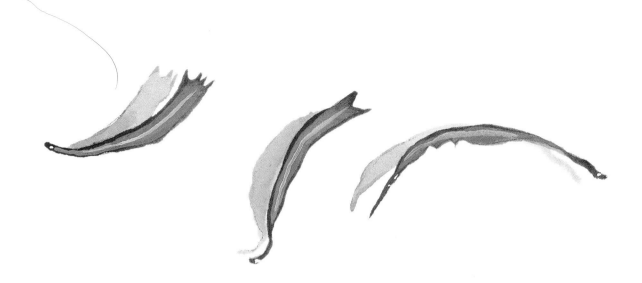

For Timothy Davis Tarangelo, with love
—S.K.

In memory of my parents, who (usually) tolerated
the creatures I brought home, and encouraged my
interest in living things of all stripes and spots

—S.S.

PET SELECTION

I wanted a dog.
Mom said, "Too **loud.**"

I wanted a snake.
Mom said, "Too *scary.*"

I wanted a horse.
Mom said, "Too BIG."

All I could get
was a guinea pig.

NAME

He's soft,
     plump,
       fuzzy,
         brown
—like a teddy bear.

So I name him
Theodore.

DANGER

When I bring more hay
for his bed,

Theodore
jerks his head

and presses himself
to the floor.

It's only me,
Theodore.

NOT HUNGRY

The food I put
in Theodore's dish

—red pellets,
    yellow pellets,
        green pellets—

looks good enough
for me to eat.

But Theodore
just hides
    under the hay.

SIZE

I'm so careful,
so quiet,
so gentle.
        But still so BIG
to a guinea pig.

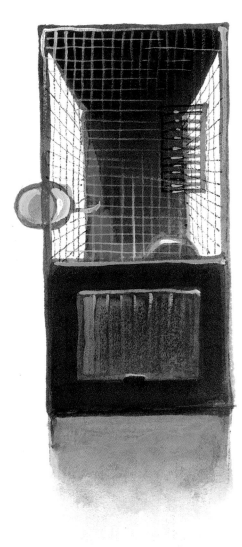

ROOMMATES

A faint whistle
in the dark.

What's that?
I listen hard.

Sleepy *wheet*,
soft *chrrr*.

Tiny *peep*,
teeny *squeep*.

Theodore's telling me,
Good night.

Sleep tight,
I whisper back.

I hope
he doesn't snore.

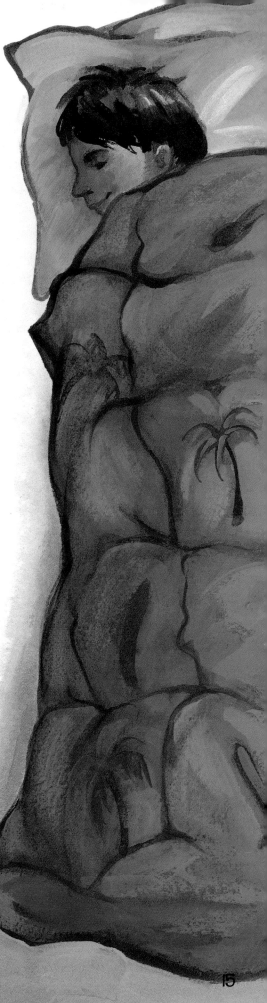

MORNING

Theodore stretches
his hind legs.
Hello, morning.

Theodore gnaws
the edge of his cage.
Hello, home.

Theodore sees me
coming close.
Goodbye, scary giant.

BREAKFAST

I save
my banana
for Theodore.

He eats
a little piece

and leaves
the rest
for me.

Who says
he's a pig?

NOISES

When I laugh too loud,
Theodore jumps.

When Dad slams the door,
Theodore runs.

Theodore hates
loud noises

     —unless
he makes them himself.

STATUE

When Theodore's busy,
I tiptoe close.

When he looks up,
I freeze.

When he doesn't hide,
I smile.

But I don't
     move
     any
     thing
     else.

CONVERSATION

I talk to Theodore
every time I pass his cage.

Hello, Theodore.
Good morning, Theodore.
How are you, Theodore?

Finally, he says,
Chut chut chut.

20

AT LAST

I offer Theodore
an apple slice.

He lets me pet
his head,

then purrs.
Hello, friend.

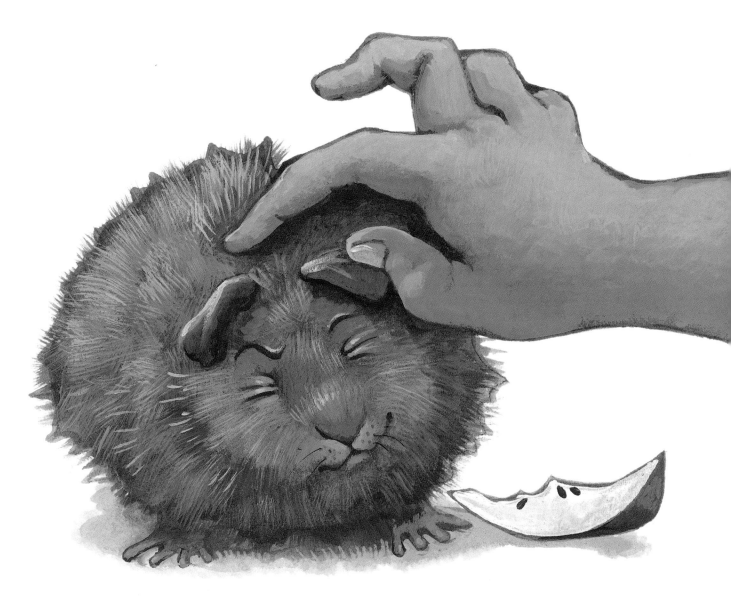

THEO-DOOR

Open
the kitchen door.
Theodore sits.

Open
the cupboard door.
Theodore sits.

But open
the refrigerator door.
Here comes Theodore!

MAGICIAN

He can't pull a rabbit
out of a hat.
Or find the ace
in a deck of cards.

But Theodore makes
a lettuce leaf
disappear—*poof!*—
like that.

EMERGENCY

When the phone rings,
Theodore jumps

and sounds the alarm:
Woooooooooooooooooooooooootz!

When the phone stops,
he sits down

and turns off his siren.

PARTY POOPER

When my friends
come to play,
Theodore hides
                under
                the
                hay.

That's okay.
        Sometimes
I'm shy too.

A GUINEA PIG TALE

Theodore doesn't have

(a tail)

When he waddles,
he wags everything.

SALARY

Tending
to a guinea pig
is work.

Feeding,
   grooming,
      cleaning,

taking him
out of his cage
to exercise.

But I get paid
   with laughs
      and hugs.

NEW HOME

Theodore loves
the grocery bag.
He travels inside it
across the floor,
a turtle with
a brown paper shell.

SLIDING BOARD

Theodore goes up
a wooden plank
step
   by step
      by step.

But he goes down
in one long

OOOOOOPS

RADIO PROGRAM

A purr, a *brrrr*,
a whistle.

A grunt, a gurgle,
a coo.

A peep, a squeak,
a *wheet-wheet-wheet*.

Today's morning
concert

On station

T-H-E-O-D-O-R-E.

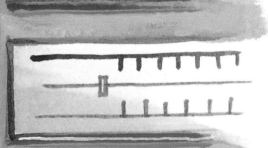

CLEANING TIME

Theodore watches me
wash his dish,
scrub his bottle,
clean out his cage.

Then he licks his paws
and rubs his face.
I guess he's trying
to help.

31

SPRING STROLL

Out to the yard
we go.

But I don't
take Theodore
for a walk.

I take him
for a sit.

LUCKY

I'm the one
who found
a four-leaf clover.

But Theodore's
the one
who ate it.

PHONE CALL

When the phone rings,
Theodore jumps,
as usual.

While I answer it,
Theodore squeals,
as usual.

Then I turn
to comfort him,
as usual.

But Theodore
    IS GONE!

COME BACK

I lean down and call,
"Theodore!"

I set a melon slice
on the floor.

I swing wide
the refrigerator door.

Then I sit down
and hug my knees.
He's my friend.
How could he leave?

SEARCH

Under the bed,
a dust bunny.

Behind the sofa,
a lost sock.

In the corner,
a spider web.

Nowhere, nowhere,
a guinea pig.

LAWN MOWER

The tiny patch
of grass
where Theodore sat
this morning
is neatly trimmed,
       —as if an elf

had mowed
his front lawn.

GONE

I can't look
at the empty cage.

No lump
under the hay.

Big lump
inside me.

ALL DAY

Nobody squeaked.
Nobody scurried.
Nobody nibbled.
Nobody smiled.

OH, THEODORE!

Someone
gnawed
the wallpaper.

Someone
chewed
the chair.

I know
it wasn't me.

DINNER

Mom's making
spaghetti,
my favorite.

But I don't want any.

She pulls out
her pot,
and it squeals:

Woooooooooooooootz!

Theodore!
Suddenly, I'm hungry.

FUR PIECE

When I set him
in my lap,

Theodore crawls
under my shirt,

tickles his way
up to my neck,

and curls himself
around me:

a brown fur collar
that purrs.

FOREVER

Theodore gurgles.
I pet him.

Theodore snuggles.
I hug him.

He's my fuzziest friend.
And I'm his biggest.